# Nannabah's Friend

MARY PERRINE

Illustrated by Leonard Weisgard

HOUGHTON
MIFFLIN
COMPANY
BOSTON

Library of Congress Cataloging-in-Publication Data

Perrine, Mary.
Nannabah's friend / Mary Perrine; illustrated by Leonard Weisgard.
p. cm.
Summary: A Navajo girl feels lonely tending sheep by herself for the first time until she makes some dolls to keep her company and, even better, meets a new friend.
ISBN 0-395-52099-1
1. Navajo Indians — Juvenile fiction. [1. Navajo Indians — Fiction. 2. Indians of North America — Southwest, New — Fiction. 3. Shepherds — Fiction.] I. Weisgard, Leonard, 1916– ill. II. Title. 89-19784
PZ7, P434Nan 1989 CIP
[E] — dc20 AC



Printed in the United States of America

RNF ISBN 0-395-52099-1
PAP ISBN 0-395-52020-7

Y 10 9 8 7 6 5 4 3 2 1

# Nannabah's Friend

BIG STAR was still looking through the round hole-for-smoke of their hogan roof, when her grandmother shook her very gently to wake her.

"Get up quickly, my grandchild," she said, "before Sun comes and finds you sleeping."

Nannabah sat on her bed made from sheepskin and stretched until the sleep was out of her eyes.

Her grandmother was taking down from a nail in their hogan wall the black pan for cooking their breakfast of bread-you-slap-with-your-hands. And from outside, Nannabah could smell the good smell of the piñon fire made by her grandfather.

When she was ready, she went outside and sat by her grandfather on his bright colored blanket.

At first, Nannabah and her grandfather sat together with quietness. Then her grandfather said, "This morning, my grandchild, I'm going to say a Navajo prayer for you. It will help when you walk alone."

Nannabah could hear her grandmother slapping dough in their hogan. She wanted to run and ask her, "My grandmother, is it today I must take your sheep alone to the canyon?" And she wanted to say, "I think you told my grandfather." But she was afraid to hear her grandmother's answer, so she stayed by the piñon fire with her grandfather.

When First Dawn began to hide the stars with whiteness, her grandfather said, "It's time, my grandchild, to say the Navajo prayer. You must listen carefully and say it after me."

He stood up and went toward the east. Nannabah went with him.

Her grandfather took white ground corn from a buckskin bag and sprinkled it on the ground in four directions. Then he began to say the prayer for Nannabah.

*Today the feet of White Corn will be mine,*
*The body of White Corn will be mine,*
*The mind of White Corn will be mine.*

He waited for Nannabah to say it. Then he went on.

*With White Corn's feet, I will walk in beauty,*
*With White Corn's body, my body will be beautiful,*
*With White Corn's mind, my thoughts will be beautiful,*
*Beauty will be in front of me, and behind me, and under me,*
*and above me, and all around me.*

Nannabah said it with shyness, but very carefully.

When they went back to the piñon fire, she sat close to her grandfather on his bright colored blanket. "Thank you, my grandfather," she said.

Her grandmother was kneeling by the fire, cooking round thin pieces of dough, and Nannabah tried to see her eyes. But she didn't look at Nannabah until after they began to eat.

Then her grandmother looked at her with gentleness, and Nannabah knew she was going to say it. "Today, my grandchild, I won't go with you when you take the sheep."

Nannabah wanted to hide her face with her hands, and she tried. But her grandmother and grandfather must have seen through her fingers.

"Don't cry, my grandchild," her grandmother said. And her grandfather put his hand on her shoulder with kindness.

Then it was time to take the sheep to the canyon. Her grandmother opened the gate for the sheep, and handed Nannabah a stick to drive them. And from the scarf that was tied to her belt she took a can with little rocks in it, and gave it to Nannabah. Nannabah looked at her, but she didn't smile or look at Nannabah.

Soon her grandmother began to pick up wood by the sheep's corral, and then she went to the hogan with the wood.

Nannabah hit the sheep very gently with her grandmother's stick, and started them up the trail to the mesa. She kept looking back, and from the top of the mesa she looked back for a long time. Her grandmother was busy piling wood by their hogan door, and then she went inside and stayed there.

After a while Nannabah hit the sheep again with her grandmother's stick and started them down the trail on the other side of the mesa. Tall rocks were on both sides, and for a long time the sheep walked slowly on the trail.

Then a big sheep with horns left the trail and went toward a clump of grass under a rock, and the others began to follow. Nannabah ran after the big sheep with horns and hit it with a stick, but it went around her.

Soon it started up the hill behind the rock, and the others followed. Nannabah went in front of them and tried to push them with her foot. But she wasn't strong enough.

Then she thought of the can with little rocks in it, which she had put in her scarf and tied to her belt. She didn't want to hear the noise, but she took the can from her scarf and shook it.

In the quietness, the noise in Nannabah's hand was loud. As if they had heard a snake, the sheep stopped moving. Then, slowly, they turned and walked away from Nannabah, and soon they were going down the trail again.

One more time, when they had come, almost, to the canyon's flat ground, the big sheep with horns started from the trail, and two others began to follow. But Nannabah went ahead of them, and rattled the can with little rocks in it, and they went back.

Finally, they were in the canyon. There was a place near the canyon's end where water fell from rocks and made a pool below. Around the water, grass was green and deep. The sheep stopped there, and began to graze, and Nannabah sat down by them in the grass.

For a long time she watched the water that was running down the rocks. And she listened to its sound. Then she looked up at the sky and clouds.

Along both sides of the canyon, the sky stood behind tall rocks. But at the canyon's end, there were no rocks for it to stand behind. And in that place, the sky came so close to her grandmother's sheep, the low white clouds and the sheep were together.

Nannabah and a crow that was going through the air and would soon be gone were alone.

She thought about her grandmother and grandfather. And she thought about her mother and father, and her little sister and baby brother, who were in their hogan that was far away. She was going to hide her eyes with her hands and cry, but she had never cried alone before. She had never been alone before.

She stood up and began to walk among the sheep by the water. Red mud was by the edge of the pool, and Nannabah touched the mud with her fingers to feel its softness. Then, an idea came to her.

She filled her hand with red mud. Using a stick to help her fingers shape the mud, she made a doll. When it was finished, the doll had a blouse and a long skirt like Nannabah's own. She named it "Little Sister."

Then she dug more mud and made another doll. This doll was a baby in a cradleboard, and Nannabah named it "Baby Brother."

She put Little Sister and Baby Brother on a flat rock in the sun to dry. She thought of the sheep then, and she watched them for a while. All of them were grazing in the deep grass by the water, and they were all near.

Soon Nannabah began to make a hogan for Little Sister and Baby Brother.

For the wall, she rolled red mud in her hands to make logs. Then she curved the logs made of mud until they were round like bracelets. Next she put them on top of one another, leaving a space toward the east for a door.

The roof was made from a long thin piece of mud Nannabah rolled in her hands and then coiled on the ground. It looked, she thought, like a Navajo basket that was upside-down. Before she fastened the roof on the wall, she made, with her finger, a round hole-for-smoke in the middle.

When the hogan was finished, she put Little Sister and Baby Brother on the floor inside. She sat on the ground then and looked at it. Soon she leaned down and looked inside at Little Sister and Baby Brother. It was a nice home, Nannabah thought. She wished her grandfather could sing for it to bless it.

She remembered some words from a song he had sung one time for a new hogan. She had gone with her grandmother and grandfather in their wagon. Many people were there, and everyone had listened with quietness to her grandfather's singing.

She wondered if her grandfather would mind if she gave a little blessing, by herself, for the little hogan. She thought if she told him he would only smile with gentleness.

She got a pinch of sand and sprinkled it, like corn pollen, in four directions around the little hogan. Then she looked toward the east and was going to sing. But she felt too shy. After a while, instead of singing, she said, very softly, the words she remembered.

*I have come to a home made with corn pollen,*
*I have come to a home made with rainwater,*
*I have come to a home made with all kinds of jewels,*
*I have come to a home of everlasting beauty.*

Nannabah smiled with shyness, as if someone had been listening. Then she took Little Sister and Baby Brother from the little hogan and put them on the ground outside. She was going to talk to them, but she remembered that they had no ears. And she remembered, suddenly, that she was still alone.

She looked up at Sun. Her grandmother had told her once that when it was time to start the sheep from the canyon Sun would be standing over the tallest rock. Sun was almost there. Soon Sun was there.

She put Little Sister and Baby Brother back inside the little hogan. But first she talked to them. "I'm glad," Nannabah said, "I made you from red mud, and I'm glad I made a home for you. But I wish you had ears and could hear me. And I wish you could talk to me."

Then she hit the sheep with her grandmother's stick, and started them home. Soon they were on the trail, and it wasn't long until they had come to the top of the mesa.

From the mesa, Nannabah could see her grandmother and grandfather near the hogan below. Her grandmother was weaving a rug on her loom by the door, and her grandfather was bringing corn from the wagon.

When Nannabah had come with the sheep to the end of the trail by the corral, her grandmother opened the gate and helped her drive the sheep inside.

In the morning, when her grandmother shook her to wake her, Big Star was looking again through the round hole-for-smoke. Nannabah thought first about Little Sister and Baby Brother in the little hogan. Big Star, she thought, must be looking at them too. And there was no one to wake them.

When her grandmother had made their bread-you-slap-with-your-hands Nannabah ate with her grandmother and grandfather. Then she went to the corral. Her grandmother opened the gate for the sheep, and Nannabah started them up to the mesa.

On the other side of the mesa, tall rocks hid the canyon's floor. Nannabah looked between some of them trying to see the little hogan, but other tall rocks stood behind. Then, near the end of the trail, one rock was low, and Nannabah ran ahead of the sheep, and climbed up on it.

She could see the little hogan — and something else. Sheep were grazing in the grass by the water, and a girl was sitting near the little hogan — a real girl.

Nannabah wanted to run ahead of her sheep again. But she was afraid. She wondered if the girl would smile and talk to her and listen when she talked.

When Nannabah's sheep came, at last, to the green grass, Nannabah and the other girl looked at each other with shyness.

Nannabah sat down and took Little Sister and Baby Brother from the little hogan and laid them, gently, on the ground outside. Then she put Baby Brother in her lap, and she handed Little Sister to the other girl to hold in her lap.

The girl smiled then, and talked. "When I saw the dolls and the little hogan," she said, "I wished the girl who made them would come back and be my friend."

Then Nannabah smiled. "I think," she said, "I made Little Sister and Baby Brother because I wished that *you* would come and be *my* friend."

When Sun stood over the tallest rock Nannabah and the other girl went different ways from the canyon with their sheep.

Every morning after that, when Nannabah ran ahead of her sheep and climbed on the low rock, she saw her friend waiting by the little hogan.